HORRID HENRY MEETS THE QUEEN

Francesca Simon spent her childhood on the beach in California, and then went to Yale and Oxford Universities to study medieval history and literature. She now lives in London with her family. She has written over 50 books and won the Children's Book of the Year in 2008 at the Galaxy British Book Awards for *Horrid Henry and the Abominable Snowman*.

Also by Francesca Simon

HORRID HENRY
MEETS THE QUEEN

Francesca Simon
Illustrated by Tony Ross

Orion
Children's Books

For my childhood friends
Tootie Ackerman-Hicks and Dinah Manoff

ORION CHILDREN'S BOOKS

First published in Great Britain in 2004 by Orion Children's Books
This edition first published in 2008 by Orion Children's Books
This edition published in 2016 by Hodder and Stoughton

5

A CIP catalogue record for this book
is available from the British Library.

ISBN 978 1 4072 3040 5

Printed and bound in Great Britain
by Clays Ltd, St Ives plc

The paper and board used in this book are
made from wood from responsible sources.

Orion Children's Books
An imprint of
Hachette Children's Group
Part of Hodder and Stoughton
Carmelite House
50 Victoria Embankment
London EC4Y 0DZ

An Hachette UK Company
www.hachette.co.uk

www.hachettechildrens.co.uk

CONTENTS

1

HORRID HENRY'S CHORES

The weekend! The lovely, lovely weekend.
Sleeping in. Breakfast in his pyjamas.
Morning TV. Afternoon TV. Evening TV.
No school and no Miss Battle-Axe for two
whole days.

In fact, there was only one bad thing
about the weekend. Henry didn't even
want to think about it. Maybe Mum
would forget, he thought hopefully.
Maybe today would be the day she didn't
burst in and ruin everything.

Horrid Henry settled down in the
comfy black chair and switched on his
new favourite TV show, *Hog House*, where
teenagers competed to see whose room

was the most disgusting.

Henry couldn't wait till he was a terrible teen too. His bedroom would surely beat anything ever seen on *Hog House*.

"Eeeew," squealed Horrid Henry happily, as Filthy Phil showed off what he kept under his bed.

"Yuck!" shrieked Horrid Henry, as Mouldy Myra yanked open her cupboard.

"Oooh, gross!" howled Horrid Henry, as Tornado Tariq showed why his family had moved out.

"And this week's winner for the most revolting room is – "

CLUNK

CLUNK

CLUNK

Mum clanked in. She was dragging her favourite instruments of torture: a hoover and a duster. Peter followed.

"Henry, turn off that horrid programme

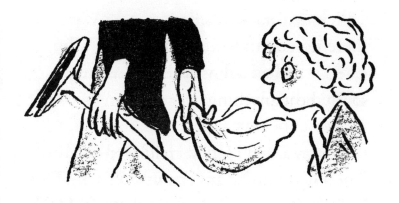

this minute," said Mum. "It's time to do your chores."

"NO!" screamed Horrid Henry.

Was there a more hateful, horrible word in the world than chores? *Chores* was worse than *homework*. Worse than *vegetables*. Even worse than *injection, share,* and *bedtime*. When he was King no child would ever have to do chores. Any parent who so much as whispered the word *chores* would get catapulted over the battlements into the piranha-infested moat.

"You can start by picking up your dirty socks from the floor," said Mum.

3

Pick up a sock? Pick up a sock? Was there no end to Mum's meanness? Who cared if he had a few old socks scattered around the place?

"I can't believe you're making me do this!" screamed Henry. He glared at Mum. Then he glared at his crumpled socks. The socks were miles away from the sofa. He'd pick them up later. Much later.

"Henry, your turn to hoover the sitting room," said Mum. "Peter, your turn to dust."

"No!" howled Horrid Henry. "I'm allergic to hoovers."

Mum ignored him.

"Then empty the bins and put the dirty clothes into the washing machine. And make sure you separate the whites from the coloureds."

Henry didn't move.

"It will only take fifteen minutes," said Mum.

"It's not fair!" wailed Henry. "I hoovered last week."

"No you didn't, I did," said Peter.

"I did!" screamed Henry.

"Liar!"

"Liar!"

"Can't I do it later?" said Horrid Henry. Later had such a happy way of turning into never.

"N–O spells no," said Mum.

Peter started dusting the TV.

"Stop it!" said Henry. "I'm watching."

"I'm dusting," said Peter.

"Out of my way, worm," hissed Horrid Henry.

Mum marched over and switched off the TV. "No TV until you do your chores, Henry. Everyone has to pitch in and help in this family."

Horrid Henry was outraged. Why should he help around the house? That was his lazy parents' job. Didn't he work hard enough already, heaving his heavy bones to school every day?

And all the schoolwork he did! It was amazing, thought Horrid Henry, as he lay kicking and screaming on the sofa, that he was still alive.

"I WON'T! I'M NOT YOUR SLAVE!"

"Henry, it's not fair if Mum and Dad do *all* the housework," said Perfect Peter.

That seemed fair to Henry.

"Quite right Peter," said Mum, beaming. "What a lovely thoughtful boy you are."

"Shut up, Peter!" screamed Henry.

"Don't be horrid, Henry!" screamed Mum.

"No TV and no pocket money until you
do your chores," said Dad, running in.

Henry stopped screaming.

No pocket money! No TV!

"I don't need any pocket money,"
shrieked Henry.

"Fine," said Mum.

Wait, what was he saying?

Of course he needed pocket money.
How else would he buy sweets? And he'd
die if he couldn't watch TV.

"I'm calling the police," said Horrid
Henry. "They'll come and arrest you for
child cruelty."

"Finished!" sang out Perfect Peter. "I've
done all *my* chores," he added, "can I have
my pocket money please?"

"Of course you can," said Mum. She
handed Peter a shiny 50p piece.

Horrid Henry glared at Peter. Could that
ugly toad get any uglier?

"All right," snarled Henry. "I'll hoover.

7

And out of my way, frog face, or I'll hoover
you up."

"Mum!" wailed Peter. "Henry's trying to
hoover me."

"Just do your chores, Henry," said Mum.
She felt tired.

"You could have done *all* your chores in
the time you've spent arguing," said Dad.
He felt tired, too.

Henry slammed the sitting room door
behind his mean horrible parents. He
looked at the hoover with loathing. Why
didn't that stupid machine just hoover by
itself? A robot hoover, that's what he
needed.

Henry switched it on.

VROOM! VROOM!

"Hoover, hoover!" ordered Henry.

The hoover did not move.

"Go on, hoover, you can do it," said Henry.

VROOM! VROOM! Still the hoover didn't move.

What a lot of noise that stupid machine makes, thought Henry. I bet you can hear it all over the house.

And then suddenly Horrid Henry had a brilliant, spectacular idea. Why had he never thought of it before? He'd ask to hoover every week.

Henry dragged the hoover over to the sitting room door and left it roaring there. Then he flopped on the sofa and switched

on the TV. Great, *Hog House* hadn't
finished!

VROOMVROOMVROOM

Mum and Dad listened to the hoover
blaring from the sitting room. Goodness,
Henry was working hard. They were
amazed.

"Isn't Henry doing a good job," said
Mum.

"He's been working over thirty minutes
non-stop," said Dad.

"Finally, he's being responsible," said
Mum.

"At last," said Dad.

"Go Tariq!" cheered Henry, as Tornado
Tariq blew into his parents' tidy bedroom.
Ha ha ha, chortled Henry, what a shock
those parents would get.

"Stay tuned for the Filthy Final between
Tariq and Myra, coming up in three

minutes!" said the presenter, Dirty Dirk.

Footsteps. Yikes, someone was coming. Oh no.

Henry sprang from the sofa, turned off the telly and grabbed the hoover.

Mum walked in.

Horrid Henry began to pant.

"I've worked so hard, Mum," gasped Henry. "Please can I stop now?"

Mum stared at the dustballs covering the carpet.

"But Henry," said Mum. "There's still dust everywhere."

"I can't help it," said Henry. "I did my best."

"All right, Henry," said Mum, sighing.

YES! thought Horrid Henry.

"But remember, no TV until you've emptied the bins and separated the laundry."

"I know, I know," muttered Henry, running up the stairs. If he finished his chores in the next two minutes, he'd be in time for the *Hog House* final!

Right. Mum said to empty the bins. She didn't say into what, just that the bins had to be empty.

It was the work of a few moments to tip all the wastepaper baskets onto the floor.

That's done, thought Horrid Henry, racing down the stairs. Now that stupid laundry. When he was a billionaire computer game tester, he'd never wash his clothes. He'd just buy new ones.

Horrid Henry glared at the dirty clothes piled on the floor in front of the washing machine. It would take him hours to separate the whites from the coloureds. What a waste of his valuable time, thought Henry. Mum and Dad just made him do it

to be mean. What difference could it make
to wash a red sweatshirt with a white
sheet? None.

Horrid Henry shoved all the clothes into
the washing machine and slammed the
door.

Free at last.

"Done!" shrieked Horrid Henry.

★

Wow, what a brilliant *Hog House* that was,
thought Horrid Henry, jingling his pocket
money. He wandered past the washing
machine. Strange, he didn't remember all
those pink clothes swirling around. Since
when did his family have pink sheets and
pink towels?

Since he'd washed a red sweatshirt with
the whites.

Uh oh.

Mum would be furious. Dad would be
furious. His punishment would be terrible.
Hide! thought Horrid Henry.

★

Dad stared at his newly pink underpants,
shirts, and vests.

Mum stared at her best white skirt, now
her worst pink one.

Henry stared at the floor. This time there
was no escape.

"Maybe we're asking too much of you,"
said Dad, gazing at the trail of rubbish
lying round the house.

"You're just not responsible enough,"
said Mum.

"Too clumsy," said Dad.

"Too young," said Mum.

"Maybe it's easier if we do the chores ourselves," said Dad.

"Maybe it is," said Mum.

Horrid Henry could hardly believe his ears. No more chores? Because he was so bad at doing them?

"Yippee!" squealed Henry.

"On the other hand, maybe not," said Dad, glaring. "We'll see how well you do your chores next week."

"Okay," said Horrid Henry agreeably.

He had the feeling his chore-doing skills wouldn't be improving.

2

MOODY MARGARET CASTS A SPELL

"You are getting sleepy," said Moody Margaret. "You are getting very sleepy ..."

Slowly she waved her watch in front of Susan.

"So sleepy ... you are now asleep ... you are now fast asleep ..."

"No I'm not," said Sour Susan.

"When I click my fingers you will start snoring."

Margaret clicked her fingers.

"But I'm not asleep," said Susan.

Margaret glared at her.

"How am I supposed to hypnotise you if you don't try?" said Margaret.

"I *am* trying, you're just a bad hypnotist,"

said Susan sourly. "Now it's my turn."

"No it's not, it's still mine," said Margaret.

"You've had your go," said Susan.

"No I haven't!"

"But I never get to be the hypnotist!" wailed Susan.

"Cry baby!"
"Meanie!"
"Cheater!"
"Cheater!"
Slap!
Slap!

Susan glared at Margaret. Why was she friends with such a mean moody bossyboots?

Margaret glared at Susan. Why was she friends with such a stupid sour sulker?

"I hate you, Margaret!" screamed Sour Susan.

"I hate you more!" screamed Moody Margaret.

18

"Shut up, landlubbers!" shrieked Horrid Henry from his hammock in the garden next door. "Or the Purple Hand will make you walk the plank!"

"Shut up yourself, Henry," said Margaret.

"Yeah, Henry," said Susan.

"You are stupid, you are stupid," chanted Rude Ralph, who was playing pirates with Henry.

"You're the stupids," snapped Moody Margaret. "Now leave us alone, we're busy."

"Henry, can I play pirates with you?" asked Perfect Peter, wandering out from the house.

"No, you puny prawn!" screamed Captain Hook. "Out of my way before I tear you to pieces with my hook!"

"Muuum," wailed Peter. "Henry said he was going to tear me to pieces!"

"Stop being horrid, Henry!" shouted Mum.

"And he won't let me play with him," said Peter.

"Can't you be nice to your brother for once?" said Dad.

NO! thought Horrid Henry. Why should he be nice to that tell-tale brat?

Horrid Henry did not want to play pirates with Peter. Peter was the world's worst pirate. He couldn't swordfight. He couldn't swashbuckle. He couldn't remember pirate curses. All he could do was whine.

"Okay, Peter, you're the prisoner. Wait in the fort," said Henry.

"But I'm always the prisoner," said Peter.

Henry glared at him.

"Do you want to play or don't you?"

"Yes Captain," said Peter. He crawled into the lair of the Purple Hand. Being prisoner was better than nothing, he supposed. He just hoped he wouldn't have to wait too long.

"Let's get out of here quick," Henry whispered to Rude Ralph. "I've got a great idea for playing a trick on Margaret and Susan." He whispered to Ralph. Ralph grinned.

Horrid Henry hoisted himself onto the low brick wall between his garden and Margaret's.

Moody Margaret was still waving her watch at Susan. Unfortunately, Susan had her back turned and her arms folded.

"Go away, Henry," ordered Margaret.

"Yeah Henry," said Susan. "No boys."

"Are you being hypnotists?" said Henry.

"Margaret's trying to hypnotise me, only she can't 'cause she's a rubbish hypnotist," said Susan.

"That's your fault," said Margaret, glaring.

"Of course you can't hypnotise her," said Henry. "You're doing it all wrong."

"And what would you know about that?" asked Margaret.

"Because," said Horrid Henry, "I am a master hypnotist."

Moody Margaret laughed.

"He is too a master hypnotist," said Ralph. "He hypnotises me all the time."

"Oh yeah?" said Margaret.

"Yeah," said Henry.

"Prove it," said Margaret.

"Okay," said Horrid Henry. "Gimme the watch."

Margaret handed it over.

He turned to Ralph.

"Look into my eyes," he ordered.

Ralph looked into Henry's eyes.

"Now watch the watch," ordered Henry the hypnotist, swinging the watch back and forth. Rude Ralph swayed.

"You will obey my commands," said Henry.

"I – will – obey," said Ralph in a robot voice.

"When I whistle, you will jump off the

wall," said Henry. He whistled.

Ralph jumped off the wall.

"See?" said Horrid Henry.

"That doesn't prove he's hypnotised," said Margaret. "You have to make him do silly things."

"Like what?" said Henry.

"Tell him he's got no clothes on."

"Ralph, you're a nudie," said Henry.

Ralph immediately started running round the garden shrieking.

"Aaaaaaarrgghh!" yelped Ralph. "I'm a nudie! I'm a nudie! Give me some clothes, help help! No one look, I'm naked!"

Margaret hesitated. There was no way Henry could have *really* hypnotised Ralph – was there?

"I still don't believe he's hypnotised," said Margaret.

"Then watch this," said Horrid Henry. "Ralph – when I snap my fingers you will be . . . Margaret."

Snap!

"My name is Margaret," said Ralph. "I'm a mean bossyboots. I'm the biggest bossiest boot. I'm a frogface."

Margaret blushed red.

Susan giggled.

"It's not funny," snapped Margaret. *No one* made fun of her and lived to tell the tale.

"See?" said Henry. "He obeys my every command."

"Wow," said Susan. "You really are a hypnotist. Can you teach me?"

"Maybe," said Horrid Henry. "How much will you pay me?"

"He's just a big faker," said Margaret. She stuck her nose in the air. "If you're such a great hypnotist, then hypnotise *me*."

Oops. Now he was trapped. Margaret was trying to spoil his trick. Well, no way would he let her.

Horrid Henry remembered who he was. The boy who got Miss Battle-Axe sent to the head. The boy who terrified the bogey babysitter. The boy who tricked the Tooth Fairy. He could hypnotise Margaret any day.

"Sure," he said, waving the watch in front of Margaret.

"You are getting sleepy," droned Henry. "You are getting very sleepy. When I snap

my fingers you will obey my every command."

Henry snapped his fingers. Margaret glared at him.

"Well?" said Moody Margaret.

"Don't you know *anything*?" said Horrid Henry. He thought fast. "That was just the beginning bit. I will complete part two once I have freed Ralph from my power. Ralph, repeat after me, 'I am sellotape'."

"I am sellotape," said Rude Ralph. Then he belched.

"I am burping sellotape," said Rude Ralph. He caught Henry's eye. They burst out laughing.

"Ha ha, Susan, fooled you!" shrieked Henry.

"Did not," shrieked Susan.

"Did too. Nah nah ne nah nah!" Henry and Ralph ran round Margaret, whooping and cheering.

"Come on Margaret," said Susan. "Let's

go do some *real* hypnosis."

Margaret didn't move.

"Come on, Margaret," said Susan.

"I am sellotape," said Margaret.

"No you're not," said Susan.

"Yes I am," said Margaret.

Henry and Ralph stopped whooping.

"There's something wrong with Margaret," said Susan. "She's acting all funny. Margaret, are you okay? Margaret? Margaret?"

Moody Margaret stood very still. Her eyes looked blank.

Horrid Henry snapped his fingers.

"Raise your right arm," he ordered.

Margaret raised her right arm.

Huh? thought Horrid Henry.

"Pinch Susan."

Margaret pinched Susan.

"Owww!" yelped Susan.

"Repeat after me, 'I am a stupid girl'."

"I am a stupid girl," said Margaret.

"No you're not," said Susan.

"Yes I am," said Margaret.

"She's hypnotised," said Horrid Henry. He'd actually hypnotised Moody Margaret. This was amazing. This was fantastic. He really truly was a master hypnotist!

"Will you obey me, slave?"

"I will obey," said Margaret.

"When I click my fingers, you will be a . . . chicken."

Click!

"Squawk! Squawk! Squawk!" cackled Margaret, flapping her arms wildly.

"What have you done to her?" wailed Sour Susan.

29

"Wow," said Rude Ralph. "You've hypnotised her."

Horrid Henry could not believe his luck. If he could hypnotise Margaret, he could hypnotise anyone. Everyone would have to obey his commands. He would be master of the world! The universe! Everything!

Henry could see it now.

"Henry, ten out of ten," Miss Battle-Axe would say. "Henry is so clever he doesn't ever need to do homework again."

Oh boy, would he fix Miss Battle-Axe.

He'd make her do the hula in a grass skirt when she wasn't running round the playground mooing like a cow.

He'd make the head Mrs Oddbod just have chocolate and cake for school dinners. And no P.E. – ever. In fact,

he'd make Mrs Oddbod close down the
school.

And as for Mum and Dad ...

"Henry, have as many sweets as you like,"
Dad would say.

"No bedtime for you," Mum would say.

"Henry, watch as much TV as you want,"
Dad would say.

"Henry, here's your pocket money –

31

£1000 a week. Tell us if you need more," Mum would smile.

"Peter, go to your room and stay there for a year!" Mum and Dad would scream.

Henry would hypnotise them all later. But first, what should he make Margaret do?

Ah yes. Her house was filled with sweets and biscuits and fizzy drinks – all the things Henry's horrible parents never let him have.

"Bring us all your sweets, all your biscuits and a Fizzywizz drink."

"Yes, master," said Moody Margaret.

Henry stretched out in the hammock. So did Rude Ralph. This was the life!

Sour Susan didn't know what to do. On the one hand, Margaret was mean and horrible, and she hated her. It was fun watching her obey orders for once. On the other hand, Susan would much rather Margaret was *her* slave than Henry's.

"Unhypnotise her, Henry," said Sour Susan.

"Soon," said Horrid Henry.

"Let's hypnotise Peter next," said Ralph.

"Yeah," said Henry. No more telling tales. No more goody goody vegetable-eating I'm Mr Perfect. Oh boy would he hypnotise Peter!

Moody Margaret came slowly out of her house. She was carrying a large pitcher and a huge bowl of chocolate mousse.

"Here is your Fizzywizz drink, master," said Margaret. Then she poured it on top of him.

"Wha? Wha?" spluttered Henry, gasping and choking.

"And your dinner, frogface," she added, tipping the mousse all over Ralph.

"Ugggh!" wailed Ralph.

"NAH NAH NE NAH NAH," shrieked Margaret. "Fooled you! Fooled you!"

Perfect Peter crept out of the Purple-

Hand Fort. What was all that yelling? It must be a pirate mutiny!

"Hang on pirates, here I come!" shrieked Peter, charging at the thrashing hammock as fast as he could.

CRASH!

A sopping wet pirate captain and a mousse-covered first mate lay on the ground. They stared up at their prisoner.

"Hi Henry," said Peter. "I mean, hi

Captain." He took a step backwards. "I mean, Lord High Excellent Majesty." He took another step back.

"Ugh, we were playing pirate mutiny – weren't we?"

"DIE, WORM!" yelled Horrid Henry, leaping up.

"MUUUUUUM!" shrieked Peter.

3

HORRID HENRY'S BATHTIME

Horrid Henry loved baths.

He loved causing great big tidal waves.

He loved making bubble-bath beards and bubble-bath hats.

He loved staging battles with Yellow Duck and Snappy Croc. He loved diving for buried treasure, fighting sea monsters, and painting the walls with soapy suds.

But best of all, being in the bath meant Peter couldn't bother him, or wreck his games or get him into trouble.

Henry stretched out in the lovely warm water. The bubbles were piled high to overflowing, just as he liked.

SLOSH

SLOSH

SLOSH

A bucketload of soapy suds cascaded onto the floor. Yippee! The first tidal wave of the day. Good thing Mum wasn't around. But then what Mum didn't know wouldn't hurt her.

Now what to do first? A Croc and Duck fight? Or the killer tidal wave?

"Heh heh heh," cackled Horrid Henry, "watch your tail Yellow Duck, 'cause Snappy Croc is on the attack. Snap! Snap! Snap!"

Suddenly the bathroom door opened. A slimy toad slithered in.

"Oy, get out of here, Peter," said Henry.

"Dad said we had to share a bath," said Perfect Peter, taking off his shirt.

What?

"Liar!" screeched Horrid Henry. "You are dead meat!" He reached for his Super Soaker. Henry was not allowed to use it in the house, but this was an emergency.

"AAARRRGGGHHH," squealed Peter as a jet of water hit him in the face.

Dad dashed in.

"Put that Super Soaker away or I'll confiscate it," shouted Dad.

Henry's finger trembled on the trigger.

Dad's red face was so tempting . . .

Henry could see it now. POW! Dad soaking wet. Dad screaming. Dad snatching Super Soaker and throwing it in the rubbish and telling Henry no TV for ever . . .

Hmmm. Dad's red face was a little less tempting.

"Just look at this floor, Henry," said Dad. "What a waste of water."

"It's not a waste," said Horrid Henry, holding tight onto his Super Soaker in case Dad lunged, "it's a tidal wave."

"Too much water is being wasted in this

house," said Dad. "From now on you and Peter will share a bath."

Horrid Henry could not believe his ears. *Share* a bath? *Share* a bath with stupid smelly Peter?

"NOOOO," wailed Henry.

"I don't mind sharing, Dad," said Peter. "We all have to do our bit to save water."

"But Peter pees in the bath," said Henry.

"I do not," said Perfect Peter. "Henry does."

"Liar!"

"Liar!"

"And we'll be squashed!" wailed Henry. "And he likes the bath too cold ! And he – "

"That's enough Henry," said Dad. "Now make room for Peter."

Horrid Henry ducked his head under water. He was never coming back up. Never. Then they'd be sorry they made him share his bath with an ugly toad snot face telltale goody-goody poo breath …

GASP.

Horrid Henry came up for air.

"If you don't make room for Peter you'll be getting out now," said Dad. "And no TV for a week."

Scowling, Horrid Henry moved his legs a fraction of an inch.

"Henry . . . " said Dad.

Horrid Henry moved his legs another fraction.

"I don't want to sit by the taps," said Peter. "They hurt my back."

"Well I don't want to sit there either," said Henry. "And I was here first. I'm not moving."

"Just get in, Peter," said Dad.

Perfect Peter got in the bath and sat against the taps. His lower lip trembled.

Ha ha ha, thought Horrid Henry, stretching out his legs. Peter was all squished at the yucky end of the bath. Good. Serve him right for ruining Henry's fun.

"Nah Nah Ne Nah Nah," chortled
Horrid Henry.

"Dad, the bath's too hot," moaned Peter.
"I'm boiling."

Dad added cold water.

"Too cold!" screeched Horrid Henry.
"I'm freezing!"

Dad added hot water.

"Too hot!" said Perfect Peter.

Dad sighed.

"New house rule: the person who sits by

the taps decides the temperature," said
Dad, letting in a trickle of cold water.
"Now I don't want to hear another peep
out of either of you," he added, closing the
door.

Horrid Henry could have punched
himself. Why hadn't he thought of that? If
he were by the taps *he'd* be the bath king.

"Move," said Henry.

"No," said Peter.

"I want to sit by the taps," said Henry.

"Too bad," said Peter. "I'm not moving."

"Make it hotter," ordered Henry.

"No," said Peter. "I control the
temperature because *I'm* sitting by the
taps."

"DAD!" shouted Henry. "Peter wants the
bath too cold!"

"MUM!" shouted Peter. "Henry wants
the bath too hot!"

"I'm freezing!"

"I'm boiling!"

"Be quiet both of you," screamed Dad from the kitchen.

Horrid Henry glared at Peter.

Perfect Peter glared at Henry.

"Move your legs," said Henry.

"I'm on my side," said Peter.

Henry kicked him.

"No you're not," said Henry.

Peter kicked him back.

Henry splashed him.

"Muuuuuuuum!" shrieked Peter. "Henry's being horrid."

"Peter's being horrid!"

"Make him stop!" shouted Henry and Peter.

45

"AAARRRRGHHHHHH!" screeched Peter.

"AAARRRRGHHHHHH!" screeched Henry.

"Stop fighting!" screamed Mum.

Perfect Peter picked up Yellow Duck.

"Give me Yellow Duck," hissed Henry.

"No," said Peter.

"But it's my duck!"

"Mine!"

SLAP

SLAP

"Waaaaaah," wailed Peter. "Muuuum!"

Mum ran in. "What's going on in here?"

"He hit me!" screeched Henry and Peter.

"That's it, both of you out," said Mum.

★

"Bathtime, boys," said Mum the next evening.

Horrid Henry raced upstairs. This time he'd make sure he was the first one in. But

when he reached the bathroom, a terrible
sight met his eyes. There was Peter, already
sitting at the tap end. Henry could practic-
ally see the ice cubes floating on the
freezing water.

Rats. Another bathtime ruined.

Henry stuck his toe in.

"It's too cold!" moaned Henry. "And I
don't want to have a bath with Peter. I
want my own bath."

"Stop making a fuss and get in," said Mum. "And no fighting. I'm leaving the door open."

Horrid Henry got into the bath.

Eeeeek! He was turning into an icicle! Well, not for long. He had a brilliant, spectacular plan.

"Stop making ripples," hissed Horrid Henry. "You have to keep the water smooth."

"I am keeping the water smooth," said Peter.

"Shh! Hold still."

"Why?" said Peter.

"I wouldn't splash if I were you," whispered Henry. "*It* doesn't like splashing."

"Why are you whispering?" said Peter.

"Because there's a monster in the tub," said Henry.

"No there isn't," said Peter.

"It's the plughole monster," said Horrid

Henry. "It sneaks up
the drains, slithers
through the
plughole and –
slurp! Down you
go."

"You big liar," said
Peter. He shifted slightly off the plughole.

Henry shrugged.

"It's up to you," he said. "Don't say I
didn't warn you when the Plughole
Monster sucks you down the drain!"

Peter scooted away from the plughole.

"MUUUUM!" he howled, jumping out
of the bath. Henry grabbed his spot,
turned on the hot water, and stretched out.
Ahhhh!

Peter continued to shriek.

"What's going on in here?" said Mum
and Dad, bursting into the bathroom.

"Henry said I was going to get sucked
down the plughole," snivelled Peter.

"Don't be horrid, Henry," said Mum. "Get out of the bath this minute."

"But – but . . . " said Horrid Henry.

"New house rules," said Mum. "From now on *I'll* run the bath and *I'll* decide the temperature."

We'll see about that, thought Horrid Henry.

The next evening, Henry sneaked into the bathroom. A thin trickle of water dribbled from the tap. The bath was just starting to fill. He felt the water.

Brrr! Freezing cold. Just how he hated it. Peter must have fiddled with the temperature. Well, no way! Henry turned up the hot tap full blast. Hot water gushed into the bath. That's much better, thought Horrid Henry. He smiled and went downstairs.

From his bedroom, Peter heard Henry stomping from the bathroom. What was he up to? When the coast was clear, Peter tiptoed into the bathroom and dipped his fingers in the water. Oww! Boiling hot. Just how he hated it. Henry must have fiddled with the temperature: Mum would *never* make it so hot. Peter turned up the cold tap full blast. Much better, thought Peter.

Mum and Dad were sitting in the kitchen drinking tea.

Mum smiled. "It's lovely and quiet upstairs, isn't it?"

Dad smiled. "I knew they'd be able to share a bath, in the end."

Mum stopped smiling.

"Do you hear something?"

Dad listened.

"Leave me alone!" screamed Henry from the sitting room.

"You leave me alone!" screamed Peter.

"Just the usual," said Dad.

"Didn't you put them in the bath?"

Dad stopped smiling. "No. Didn't you?"

Mum looked at Dad.

Dad looked at Mum.

Plink!

Plink!

Plink!

Water began to drip from the ceiling.

"I think I hear – RUNNING WATER!" screamed Mum. She dashed up the stairs.

Dad ran after her.

Mum opened the bathroom door.

Water gushed from the bathroom, and roared down the stairs.

SLIP!

SLIDE!

Mum landed on her bottom.

Plop!

Dad toppled into the bath.

Splash!

"It wasn't me!" screamed Henry.

"It wasn't me!" wailed Peter. Then he burst into tears.

"Mum!" wept Peter. "I've been a bad boy."

★

Snap! Snap!

Snappy Croc was defending his tail. Yellow Duck was twisting round to attack. Ka-boom!

Horrid Henry lay back in the bath and closed his eyes. Mum and Dad had decided to let Henry have baths on his own. To save water, they'd take showers.

4

HORRID HENRY MEETS THE QUEEN

Perfect Peter bowed to himself in the mirror.

"Your Majesty," he said, pretending to present a bouquet. "Welcome to our school, your Majesty. My name is Peter, Your Majesty. Thank you, Your Majesty. Goodbye, Your Majesty." Slowly Perfect Peter retreated backwards, bowing and smiling.

"Oh shut up," snarled Horrid Henry. He glared at Peter. If Peter said 'Your Majesty' one more time, he would, he would – Horrid Henry wasn't sure what he'd do, but it would be horrible.

The Queen was coming to Henry's school! The real live Queen! The real live Queen, with her dogs and jewels and crowns and castles and beefeaters and knights and horses and ladies-in-waiting, was coming to see the Tudor wall they had built.

Yet for some reason Horrid Henry had not been asked to give the Queen a bouquet. Instead, the head, Mrs Oddbod, had chosen Peter.

Peter!

Why stupid smelly old ugly toad Peter? It was so unfair. Just because Peter had more stars than anyone in the 'Good as

56

Gold' book, was that any reason to choose
him? Henry should have been chosen. He
would do a much better job than Peter.
Besides, he wanted to ask the Queen how
many TVs she had. Now he'd never get the
chance.

"Your Majesty," said Peter, bowing.

"Your Majesty," mimicked Henry,
curtseying.

Perfect Peter ignored him. He'd been
ignoring Henry a lot ever since *he'd* been
chosen to meet the queen. Come to think
of it, everyone had been ignoring Henry.

"Isn't it thrilling?" said Mum for the
millionth time.

"Isn't it fantastic?" said Dad for the billionth time.

"NO!" Henry had said. Who'd want to hand some rotten flowers to a stupid queen anyhow? Not Horrid Henry. And he certainly didn't want to have his picture in the paper, and everyone making a fuss.

"Bow, bouquet, answer her question, walk away," muttered Perfect Peter. Then he paused. "Or is it bouquet, bow?"

Horrid Henry had had just about enough of Peter showing off.

"You're doing it all wrong," said Henry.

"No I'm not," said Peter.

"Yes you are," said Henry. "You're supposed to hold the bouquet up to her nose, so she can have a sniff before you give it to her."

Perfect Peter paused.

"No I'm not," said Peter.

Horrid Henry shook his head sadly. "I think we'd better practice," he said.

"Pretend I'm the
Queen." He picked
up Peter's shiny
silver crown, covered
in fool's jewels, and
put it on his head.

Perfect Peter
beamed. He'd been
begging Henry to practise with him all
morning. "Ask me a question the Queen
would ask," said Peter.

Horrid Henry considered.

"Why are you so smelly, little boy?" said
the Queen, holding her nose.

"The Queen wouldn't ask *that*!" gasped
Perfect Peter.

"Yes she would," said Henry.

"Wouldn't."

"Would."

"And I'm not smelly!"

Horrid Henry waved his hand in front of
his face.

"Poo!" said the Queen. "Take this smelly boy to the Tower."

"Stop it, Henry," said Peter. "Ask me a real question, like my name or what year I'm in."

"Why are you so ugly?" said the Queen.

"MUM!" wailed Peter. "Henry called me ugly. And smelly."

"Don't be horrid, Henry!" shouted Mum.

"Do you want me to practise with you or don't you?" hissed Henry.

"Practise," sniffed Peter.

"Well, go on then," said Henry.

Perfect Peter walked up to Henry and bowed.

"Wrong!" said Henry. "You don't bow to the Queen, you curtsey."

"Curtsey?" said Peter. Mrs Oddbod hadn't said anything about curtseying. "But I'm a boy."

"The law was changed," said Henry. "Everyone curtseys now."

Peter hesitated.

"Are you sure?" asked Peter.

"Yes," said Henry. "And when you meet the Queen, you put your thumb on your nose and wriggle your fingers. Like this."

Horrid Henry cocked a snook.

Perfect Peter gasped. Mrs Oddbod hadn't said anything about thumbs on noses.

"But that's . . . rude," said Perfect Peter.

"Not to the Queen," said Horrid Henry. "You can't just say 'hi' to the Queen like she's a person. She's the Queen. There are special rules. If you get it wrong she can

61

chop off your head."

Chop off his head! Mrs Oddbod hadn't said anything about chopping off heads.

"That's not true," said Peter.

"Yes it is," said Henry.

"Isn't!"

Horrid Henry sighed. "If you get it wrong, you'll be locked up in the Tower," he said. "It's high treason to greet the Queen the wrong way. *Everyone* knows that."

Perfect Peter paused. Mrs Oddbod hadn't said anything about being locked up in the Tower.

"I don't believe you, Henry," said Peter.

Henry shrugged.

"Okay. Just don't blame me when you get your head chopped off."

Come to think of it, thought Peter, there *was* a lot of head-chopping when people met kings and queens. But surely that was just in the olden days…

"MUM!" screamed Peter.

Mum ran into the room.

"Henry said I had to curtsey to the Queen," wailed Peter. "And that I'd get my head chopped off if I got it wrong."

Mum glared at Henry.

"How *could* you be so horrid, Henry?" said Mum. "Go to your room!"

"Fine!" screeched Horrid Henry.

"I'll practise with you, Peter," said Mum.

"Bow, bouquet, answer her question, walk away," said Peter, beaming.

★

The great day arrived. The entire school lined up in the playground, waiting for the Queen. Perfect Peter, dressed in his best party clothes, stood with Mrs Oddbod by the gate.

A large black car pulled up in front of the school.

"There she is!" shrieked the children.

Horrid Henry was furious. Miss Battle-Axe had made him stand in the very last row, as far away from the Queen as he could be. How on earth could he find out if she had 300 TVs standing way back here? Anyone would think Miss Battle-Axe wanted to keep him away from the Queen on purpose, thought Henry, scowling.

Perfect Peter waited, clutching an enormous bouquet of flowers. His big moment was here.

"Bow, bouquet, answer her question, walk away. Bow, bouquet, answer her question, walk away," mumbled Peter.

"Don't worry, Peter, you'll be perfect," whispered Mrs Oddbod, urging him forward.

Horrid Henry pushed and shoved to get a closer view. Yes, there was his stupid brother, looking like a worm.

Perfect Peter walked slowly towards the Queen.

"Bow, bouquet, answer her question, walk away," he mumbled. Suddenly that didn't sound right.

Was it bow, bouquet? Or bouquet, bow?

The Queen looked down at Peter.

Peter looked up at the Queen.

"Your Majesty," he said.

Now what was he supposed to do next?

Peter's heart began to pound. His mind was blank.

Peter bowed. The bouquet smacked him in the face.

"Oww!" yelped Peter.

What had he practised? Ah yes, now he remembered!

Peter curtseyed. Then he cocked a snook.

Mrs Oddbod gasped.

Oh no, what had he done wrong?

Aaarrgh, the bouquet! It was still in his hand.

Quickly Peter thrust it at the Queen.

Smack!

The flowers hit her in the face.

"How lovely," said the Queen.

"Waaaa!" wailed Peter. "Don't chop off my head!"

There was a very long silence. Henry saw his chance.

"How many TVs have you got?" shouted Horrid Henry.

The Queen did not seem to have heard.

"Come along everyone, to the display of Tudor daub-making," said Mrs Oddbod. She looked a little pale.

"I said," shouted Henry, "how many – "
A long, bony arm yanked him away.

"Be quiet, Henry," hissed Miss Battle-Axe. "Go to the back playground like we

practised. I don't want to
hear another word
out of you."

Horrid Henry
trudged off to the
vat of daub with
Miss Battle-Axe's
beady eyes
watching his every step. It was so unfair!

When everyone was in their assigned
place, Mrs Oddbod spoke. "Your Majesty,
mums and dads, boys and girls, the Tudors
used mud and straw to make daub for their
walls. Miss Battle-Axe's class will now
show you how." She nodded to the
children standing in the vat. The school
recorder band played *Greensleeves*.

Henry's class began to stomp in the vat
of mud and straw.

"How lovely," said the Queen.

Horrid Henry stomped where he'd been
placed between Jazzy Jim and Aerobic Al.

There was a whole vat of stomping
children blocking him from the Queen,
who was seated in the front row between
Miss Battle-Axe and Mrs Oddbod. If only
he could get closer to the Queen. Then he
could find out about those TVs!

Henry noticed a tiny space between
Brainy Brian and Gorgeous Gurinder.

Henry stomped his way through it.

"Hey!" said Brian.

"Oww!" said Gurinder. "That was my foot!"

Henry ignored them.

Stomp

Stomp

Stomp

Henry pounded past Greedy Graham and Weepy William.

"Oy!" said Graham. "Stop pushing."

"Waaaaaaa!" wept Weepy William.

Halfway to the front!

Henry pushed past Anxious Andrew and Clever Clare.

"Hellllppp!" squeaked Andrew, falling over.

"Watch out, Henry," snapped Clare.

Almost there! Just Moody Margaret and Jolly Josh stood in his way.

Margaret stomped.

Josh stomped.

Henry trampled through the daub till he stood right behind Margaret.

SQUISH. SQUASH. SQUISH.
SQUASH.

"Stop stomping on my bit," hissed
Moody Margaret.

"Stop stomping on *my* bit," said Horrid
Henry.

"I was here first," said Margaret.

"No you weren't," said Henry. "Now get
out of my way."

"Make me," said Moody Margaret.

Henry stomped harder.

SQUELCH! SQUELCH! SQUELCH!

Margaret stomped harder.

STOMP! STOMP! STOMP!

Rude Ralph pushed forward. So did
Dizzy Dave.

STOMP! STOMP! STOMP!

Sour Susan pushed forward. So did
Kung-Fu Kate.

STOMP! STOMP! STOMP!
STOMP! STOMP!

A tidal wave of mud and straw flew

out of the vat.

SPLAT! Miss Battle-Axe was covered.

SPLAT! Mrs Oddbod was covered.

SPLAT! The Queen was covered.

"Oops," said Horrid Henry.

Mrs Oddbod fainted.

"How lovely," mumbled the Queen.

HORRID HENRY *is also available as an audio download and on CD, all read by Miranda Richardson*

"A hoot from beginning to end ... As always, Miranda Richardson's delivery is perfection and the manic music is a delight." *Daily Express*

"Long may this dreadful boy continue to terrorise all who know him. He's a nightmare, but so entertaining ... Miranda Richardson's spirited reading is accompanied by a brilliant music soundtrack – they make a noisy and fun-filled duo." *Parents' Guide*